Alvin

and the Unruly Elves

Alvin
and the Unruly Elves

by Ulf Löfgren

Carolrhoda Books, Inc./Minneapolis

Two days before Christmas, Alvin was doing his holiday baking. He had finished a batch of gingersnaps and was rolling out some sugar cookies when the telephone rang.

"Who could be calling," Alvin wondered, "right in the middle of my baking?" He brushed the flour off his hands and picked up the phone.

"Hello, Alvin. This is Santa Claus calling from the North Pole. I have a big problem, and I need your help."

"What's the matter?" asked Alvin.

"It's the elves," said Santa. "They are driving me crazy. They won't do a thing I tell them to do, and I was hoping that maybe you could get through to them. Can you come to the North Pole right away? I'll send my sleigh and six wolves to pick you up. They'll have you here in no time."

"Wolves!" exclaimed Alvin. "Oh, my! Couldn't you send the reindeer instead?"

"I'd better not tire out the reindeer this close to Christmas," said Santa. "See you soon!"

Early on Christmas Eve Day, Alvin heard a lot of yipping and howling outside. "Uh-oh," he said. "That doesn't sound like the neighbor's dog." When he looked out the window, he saw six hungry-looking wolves pulling a golden sleigh.

Alvin sighed. He would have to go with the wolves. He couldn't just leave them howling in his yard.

He put on his scarf and mittens and climbed into the sleigh.

When he spread the star-covered blanket around him, a ringing sound near his feet startled him. He searched under the blanket and found a portable telephone.

"Hello, this is Alvin. Who's calling?"

"It's Santa, of course. I just wanted to tell you there's a basket filled with sandwiches and a thermos of hot cocoa on the back of the sleigh."

"Great! It will get cold riding all the way to the North Pole. And I can give the wolves sandwiches if they get too hungry," said Alvin, eyeing their glistening teeth.

When Alvin and the
wolves reached the North Pole, Santa bustled out
to greet them. "I'm so glad you came, Alvin. I told
you my wolves were fast. Did you like the sandwiches?"

"Oh, yes, and the wolves especially liked the ones with pickles,"
Alvin answered. "Now, what's the problem with the elves?"

Santa looked worried. "Everything's a mess. I don't know what
to do." He shook his head. "The elves won't do a thing I tell them
to. They just keep getting into mischief. Come on, I'll show you."

In the kitchen, Mrs. Claus was baking as fast as she could. "They eat everything I make," she said to Alvin. "Just today, they've eaten all the cinnamon rolls, three dozen nut cookies, and sixteen gingerbread animals. Now they're starting on the Christmas sausages. I'm at my wit's end!"

"You can see for yourself, Alvin," said Santa. "They eat everything in sight."

Santa led Alvin to his workshop and waved his arms around. "Look at this! I still have to make some of the toys for Christmas, but I can't finish them because the elves play with them all the time. When I need my tools, they hide them from me. I haven't seen my hammer for days."

Alvin looked around, but he couldn't see the hammer either.

In the front yard, Santa turned to Alvin. "I asked them to shovel a path for my sleigh, but instead, they've built snow forts and snowcreatures, and now they're throwing snowballs. Look out, Alvin!"

SPLIT! SPLAT! The elves cheered as two soft, wet snowballs landed squarely on Santa and Alvin.

"We need to keep the house and work-shop warm and cozy, so I asked the elves to carry in some wood for the fireplace. But what do they do? They turn the log pile into a fort and play hide-and-seek."

Then they went to the barn.

"They're supposed to be mucking out the stalls. But I find them in here riding the animals and tumbling in the hay. It's terrible!"

In the dining room, everything was ready for supper, but Mrs. Claus sat all alone. "The porridge is getting cold," she sighed.

"See, Alvin. This is the way they behave at every meal," said Santa.

Alvin could see elves hiding all around the room, but not one of them would sit at the table.

Then they heard more elves
giggling in the next room.
    "Oh, no!" cried Santa.
"They've hung trash on
the Christmas tree!"

    "That does it!" yelled Alvin, hopping up and down.
"Tomorrow is Christmas, and there's no time for this nonsense.
Now trim that tree properly, and I mean NOW!"
    The elves had never seen anyone hopping mad before. Alvin's
face turned red and his eyes were squeezed tight. It was the
most fun the elves had had all day.

In fact, the elves were so impressed, they surprised everyone by doing exactly as Alvin asked. They decorated the tree with shiny glass balls and glowing candles. On top of the tree they placed a beautiful Christmas star. When they were finished, Santa was happy, and the elves felt quite proud of themselves.

"Now we're going to practice our Christmas carols, so Santa and Mrs. Claus can get some work done," Alvin told them. The elves sang in their best voices, while Santa hummed along in the workshop and Mrs. Claus joined the chorus from the kitchen.

The next morning, they all helped to ring in Christmas Day with the special Christmas bell. Santa could hear its mighty ring as he returned to the North Pole.

Then it was the elves' turn to open their Christmas presents. Santa and Mrs. Claus watched in amazement as the elves thanked Alvin politely and played nicely with their toys.

As it grew dark outside, Alvin lit the candles on the Christmas tree. Then he called for everyone to join hands and dance around the tree. They danced, singing and laughing, until they were too tired to dance another step.

Finally, Alvin told the elves it was time to go to bed.

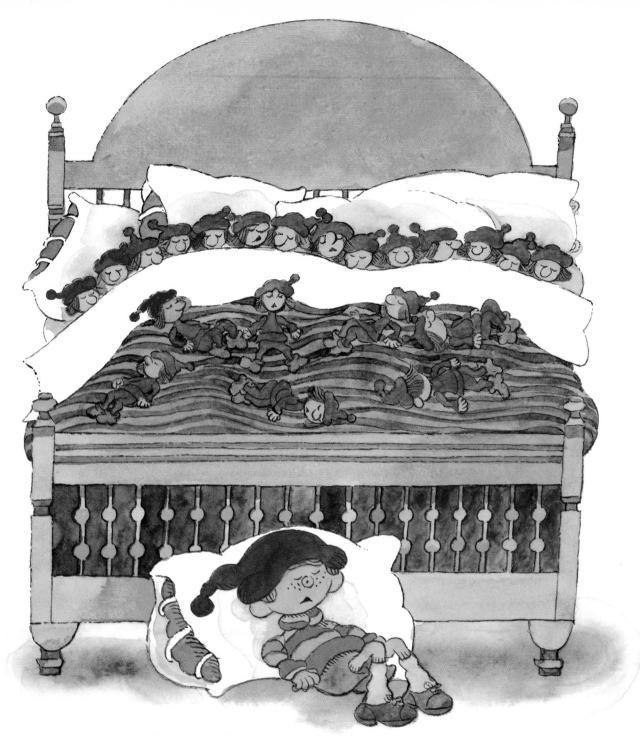

The elves piled into their big feather bed. Alvin curled up at the bottom.

"It was a wonderful day. You all behaved very well," said Alvin. "You won't give Santa any trouble next Christmas, will you?"

There was no answer, just snores.

"Well, merry Christmas everyone," Alvin said sleepily, and soon he was snoring, too.

This edition first published 1992 by Carolrhoda Books, Inc.

Originally published by Norstedts Förlag, Stockholm.
Original edition copyright © 1991 by Ulf Löfgren under the title
ALBIN OCH DE BUSIGA TOMTARNA.

Library of Congress Cataloging-in-Publication Data

Löfgren, Ulf.
   [Albin och de busiga tomtarna. English]
   Alvin and the unruly elves / by Ulf Löfgren.
      p.   cm.
   Translation of: Albin och de busiga tomtarna.
   Summary: When Santa finds it impossible to control his
mischievous elves and stop them from ruining his workshop, he
brings Alvin to the North Pole to solve the problem.
   ISBN 0-87614-590-X
   [1. Elves—Fiction. 2. North Pole—Fiction. 3. Santa Claus—
Fiction.] I. Title.
   PZ7.L826Ad   1992
[E]—dc20   91-44303
                                                        CIP
                                                         AC

Manufactured in the United States of America

1   2   3   4   5   6   97   96   95   94   93   92